THE AMIABLE GIANT

THE
AMIABLE GIANT

BY

LOUIS SLOBODKIN

THE MACMILLAN COMPANY
NEW YORK

FOR

TWO LITTLE GIANTS

NATHAN AND DAVIE

WITH LOVE

First Printing

PRINTED IN THE UNITED STATES OF AMERICA

Published simultaneously in Canada

THE AMIABLE GIANT

There was once an amiable Giant who lived, as most giants do, in a big, black, granite castle on the top of a tremendous mountain. And since he was an amiable (really friendly) Giant and he was lonesome living all alone in his big castle, sometimes he came down from his mountain top to visit the little people who lived in the pretty village in the valley.

But the villagers did not understand the purpose of his visit. They would slam their doors in the face of the amiable Giant and shutter their windows.

"Take anything you want. Take our cattle. Take our grain. Take anything but leave us be," shouted the terror-stricken villagers from behind their locked doors.

I

When the Giant tried to explain that he did not want their cattle (since he was a vegetarian) and he did not need their grain (since he raised all the grain he wanted on the mountain top) . . . all he wanted was to visit and talk friendly talk . . . the villagers, who always clamped their hands to their ears, did not hear a word! That was because the Giant's voice was like the rumble and crash of thunder even when he spoke very softly.

Now there was one person in the village who could hear the Giant. He was a wicked man who spent most of his time cooking up strange poisonous brews which he said could work

wonders. This man pretended that he was a wizard and he was almost completely deaf. Therefore, when the Giant came down the mountain and said to the villagers, "Good morning, I just came down to pass the time of day," the wicked wizard did not clamp his hands over his ears. And although he was almost deaf he could hear the great voice of the Giant!

"That ugly Giant wants more grain," he told the villagers after the Giant went back home. "Yes, that ugly Giant wants two hundred and ten . . . no, two hundred and nineteen . . . I wrote down the exact number in this notebook . . . Yes, two hundred and nineteen bushels of corn, all the watermelon you've raised in your garden and two dozen of your best milk cows . . . and he wants you to bring all that halfway up the mountain by next Tuesday morning."

And that's just what the frightened villagers did.

It so happened that on Tuesdays the amiable Giant was very busy and he never put his nose out of his castle on that day and he never saw the frightened villagers dragging the grain and other things halfway up the mountain. The wicked Wizard

3

knew that. He knew that the amiable Giant always did his laundry on Monday and he always spent all day Tuesday ironing his gigantic sheets and shirts as big as tents . . . because he was a bachelor and he lived by himself.

On Tuesday nights, when everyone was fast asleep, the wicked Wizard with the help of his servants (all of them ex-robbers, ex-pirates, and ex-bandits) would cart away the things the villagers had brought up the mountain to a big secret cave. There they stored the grain and other things.

And so it went for many years. The Wizard became richer, the villagers became poorer and the innocent amiable Giant became lonesomer and lonesomer. Things might have gone on that way . . . the Wizard getting richer and the villagers get-

ting poorer and the amiable Giant becoming sadder and sadder because of his lonesomeness if it had not been for a little girl named Gwendolyn.

Gwendolyn was the village cobbler's granddaughter. She, like everyone else, trembled and cowered behind locked doors with her hands clamped over her ears when the Giant visited the village. But it happened that one morning Gwendolyn was playing with her doll Marguerite on the wooden cover of a dried-up well in the village square. The well had run dry so long ago there was only one man who remembered the time when it held water. That man was Gwendolyn's grandfather, the oldest man in the village.

He always said when he talked of times past, "Yes, that was just a few summers *before* the well dried up," or "Yep, that happened just three winters *after* the well dried up." Some years after the well dried up a wooden cover had been made to fit the top of it.

So much time was spent dragging children out of the dried-up well that the busy villagers took time off from their many tasks and built the wooden well cover as a time saver. Since then the children played ring-round-rosie around the well . . . follow the leader over the well . . . and constables and bandits all over the well . . . but no children fell into the well.

The old wooden cover had been jumped on by so many sturdy little feet it was well-worn and a few of the old wooden boards were rather loose.

On this particular morning Gwendolyn had sat herself and her doll Marguerite on the old well cover as she sang a lullaby.

The other village children had gone to pick the first flowers of
May up on the mountainside. Unfortunately, flowers made
Gwendolyn sneeze and even though she loved them dearly she
just loved them from a distance and never picked them.

Just as Gwendolyn was singing the fourteenth verse of a song
that she had made up, the children rushed down the mountainside, helter-skelter, dropping their flowers as they ran.

"The Giant's coming!" they screamed, "Oh, dear, the Giant's
coming down the mountain."

All the villagers promptly dropped whatever they were do-
ing and ran for home and bolted their windows and doors!

Everyone but Gwendolyn! She was so startled she stumbled
and fell backward on the old well cover and right down through
a loose board, down into the dried-up well!

Fortunately, people had used the old well like a big waste-
basket. They had thrown their old mattresses and such rub-
bish into the well before it had been covered over. And grass
and weeds had blown into it, too, so Gwendolyn was not hurt

when she landed on the bottom of the well. In fact, she even bounced once or twice.

Gwendolyn was not frightened when she found herself at the bottom of the dry well. She knew she would be found after the Giant went home again. And she knew, too, that the Giant was too big to squeeze himself into the old well. And even though his gigantic arms were long, they were not long enough to reach her at the bottom of the well. Then she thought of something that made her tremble. What if he were to see her sitting down in the well . . . and what if he were to poke at her with a stick?

She trembled so her teeth chattered at that thought and she hugged her doll Marguerite to her bosom. Fearfully she listened to the earth-shaking steps of the Giant as he walked along the village street. The sound of his steps came closer and closer and they sounded like the approach of a great storm.

Suddenly the sound of his steps stopped. The Giant had

knelt down and tapped gently at some village door as he always did when he visited the village.

Gwendolyn hugged Marguerite tighter during that sudden silence. And she forget to cover her ears as she always had done when the Giant spoke. Now, for the first time, she heard his loud booming voice. Down there at the bottom of the well his voice sounded like the mumbling roar of distant thunder.

"Anybody home?" asked the amiable Giant.

No one answered him.

"Nice weather we're having," he went on.

The frightened villagers behind their bolted doors kept their hands clamped to their ears and they all pretended they were not at home.

"I guess we could stand a little rain. . . ."

The villagers still remained silent.

"I saw the village children picking wildflowers up on the mountain," said the Giant after another moment of silence. "I have some especially fine pansies growing in one of my window boxes . . . I could bring some down for you . . . if you want them. I have very pretty purple ones."

The Giant waited a moment for someone to say something. Then he tapped on one of the shutters of the house.

"Do you hear me?" asked the Giant, raising his voice a little.

9

The frightened villagers gave up pretending they were not at home.

"Please go away," shouted one villager. Then the others joined in and from behind their locked doors and windows they wailed. "Please leave us alone . . . We can't give you any grain . . . Our crops have been bad."

"I guess you don't hear very well . . . I don't want your grain or anything you have," said the Giant, sadly, "I'll come again next week and I'll bring my purple pansies."

Then the Giant stood up and slowly walked back to his lonesome black granite castle on the top of the mountain.

When at last the sound of the Giant's great steps was lost in the distance, the villagers unlocked their doors and cautiously looked up and down the village street. Then when they saw that the Giant was really gone, they ran out of their houses and gathered in the village square.

"Oh dear, oh dear . . . What shall we do?" they all cried as they wrung their hands. "Won't that Giant ever leave us alone?"

The wicked Wizard also came bustling out of his big house. He carried the black notebook in which he said he always wrote down what the Giant had ordered. He climbed up on the cover of the old well and raised his hand above his head.

"Listen to me! Listen to me, everybody!" screamed the old Wizard. "Here's what the ugly old Giant ordered."

"One minute, please," interrupted the village cobbler, Gwendolyn's grandfather.

10

"Silence, cobbler," commanded the wicked Wizard, haughtily, "I must report to the village what the Giant has ordered . . ."

"But please . . . I must speak," insisted the cobbler. "Has anyone seen my granddaughter, Gwendolyn? She did not come in when the Giant came."

"Oh! Oh! Oh, the poor dear child," cried some of the village ladies, "The poor, poor dear, the Giant must have taken her up to his castle!"

And for the moment all the villagers forgot to worry about the Giant and everyone worried about little Gwendolyn.

Almost everyone had some idea what should be done to rescue little Gwendolyn from the Giant. Some said they ought to drag the village cannon up the mountain and bombard the Giant.

Others suggested dynamiting his big black granite castle. Suddenly everybody had become brave as they all planned to rescue Gwendolyn from the Giant.

Gwendolyn's grandfather, the village cobbler, moved away from the loud-talking villagers and sat mournfully on the stone wall of the old dry well.

"Oh, Gwendolyn, my poor little granddaughter," he moaned. "Will I ever see my poor lost Gwendolyn again?"

And from deep down in the dry well a little voice called . . .

"Grandfather . . . I am *not* lost! I'm not lost a bit. I'm down here at the bottom of the well with Marguerite. Look down. You can see me right now."

Her grandfather quickly hopped off the wall and looked down at the smiling face of Gwendolyn.

"She's here! Gwendolyn is found," he shouted, joyfully.

The villagers crowded around the well and looked down at Gwendolyn. Then some people ran off to get the long ladder that was always used to climb down into the well to carry out the children who fell into it. In a few minutes, Gwendolyn, still hugging Marguerite, was in her grandfather's arms.

12

Then the villagers, having forgotten all about the Giant, all returned to their homes.

"Here! Here!" screamed the wicked old Wizard. "You'd better wait up until I read the orders the ugly Giant gave. You know what will happen if you do not carry out his orders."

The villagers stood still in their tracks. Some of them trembled. No one had ever thought what the Giant would do if they did not carry out his orders, but they all were sure it would be something terrible . . . very terrible.

"Now then," began the wicked Wizard, as he adjusted his spectacles and opened his black notebook. "First he wants one hundred and seventy-four bushels of wheat . . . full bushels, mind you . . ."

"But we have no wheat," cried the miller. "My mill has not ground any new wheat for two weeks . . ."

The wicked Wizard went on reading as if nothing had been said.

". . . And he wants one hundred and ninety-eight bushels of barley . . . and two hundred and eighty-five . . . no, that's a three . . . yes, three hundred and eighty-five bushels of corn."

"We have no more barley and we have no more corn," protested the village farmers. "We haven't had any rain and we have no new crops . . ."

But the Wizard paid no attention to their protests and went on reading until he had completed the list of things he said the Giant had ordered.

13

". . . And you had better get them all delivered by noon next Tuesday . . . or else!" and with that the wicked Wizard snapped his black notebook shut, slowly climbed down from the top of the dry well, and stalked across the village square to his big house.

For a moment after the Wizard left them the villagers were speechless . . . What did he mean by ". . . or else!"

The village blacksmith who was also the mayor of the village stepped forward and made a short speech.

"My friends," he said, "this looks like a very serious situation. As mayor of this village, I am herewith officially calling a meeting of all the able-bodied men of this village to consider this matter. We will meet this very night in my blacksmith shop at 8 o'clock. Please be on time."

Little Gwendolyn held on tight to her grandfather's hand and listened quietly to everything that was said both by the wicked Wizard and the village blacksmith. And she did not say a word until she and her grandfather had walked all the way home and had begun to prepare supper.

"Grandfather," she said, as the old cobbler lit the fire under the soup kettle, "did you not once tell me that the Wizard is a little deaf?"

"A little deaf, did you say?" repeated the old cobbler. "Why, yes, I did say that. He never seems to hear me when I first tell him how much it will cost to mend his pointed shoes. And he can only hear me after I've shouted the cost at least three times . . . Even then he never pays as much as I ask. Yes, I would say he is a little hard of hearing."

14

"Grandfather," said Gwendolyn, slowly, "I think he is not hard of hearing. I think he is absolutely stone deaf!"

"Stone deaf, child! What makes you think that?"

"Yes, I'm sure he is stone deaf. Because he could not have heard a word that the Giant said. Marguerite and I heard everything the Giant said as we sat on the bottom of the well. He did not say one word about wanting all that wheat and all that barley and corn. In fact, he did not want the villagers to give him any wheat or anything else. Indeed, he said he wanted to give us something."

"What did he say he'd give us?"

"Purple pansies . . . that's what."

"PURPLE PANSIES!" exclaimed the old cobbler.

"Yes, grandfather . . . Beautiful purple pansies and he said he'd bring them next week. Didn't he say that, Marguerite?"

"H-m-m," said the old cobbler, thoughtfully. "Are you sure you heard him say that, child?"

"Yes, grandfather, I am sure," said Gwendolyn.

"Very well. Let us have our supper at once. Then I must go on to the meeting at the blacksmith shop. I must get there early for a private word with the mayor."

The minute the supper dishes were washed and put away the old cobbler hurried over to the blacksmith shop as fast as his old legs could carry him. None of the other villagers had arrived yet and he was able to have his private word with the black-smith, the mayor of the village.

He quickly told the blacksmith mayor what Gwendolyn had told him.

"And your granddaughter told you the Giant says he wants us to give him nothing, but that he wants to give us something?" asked the blacksmith mayor with his eyebrows high.

"Yes," said the old cobbler.

"And what does he want to give us?" asked the blacksmith mayor.

"Purple pansies," said the cobbler.

"PURPLE PANSIES!" roared the blacksmith mayor and he collapsed in a fit of laughter and sat down on his anvil. "Purple pansies! Ho, Ho, Ho. . . ." and he laughed and laughed until tears rolled down his cheeks.

16

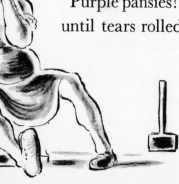

The old cobbler stood there nervously for a moment or two and then he became very angry.

"Yes! Purple pansies *is* what the Giant said!" he said, angrily. "That's what Gwendolyn said he said and my granddaughter never tells an untruth. True, she is an imaginative child but she never never tells an untruth!"

The blacksmith mayor suppressed his fit of laughter but still smiling, he patted the old cobbler on the shoulder.

"Now don't get angry, my old friend," he said. "This has been such an unfortunate day . . . and this is the first good laugh I have had. Now let us be serious. Gwendolyn said . . ."

But before he could go on the old cobbler repeated again, word for word, exactly what Gwendolyn had said.

"Now I'm not saying your granddaughter told an untruth," said the blacksmith mayor, "but as you have often said, Gwendolyn *is* an imaginative child . . . and she did tumble into the dry well. Have you thought that she might have bumped her head a little as she went tumbling down to the bottom of that well . . . And maybe that effected her hearing or her power of remembering?"

The old cobbler stroked his chin. He had not thought of that!

"Well . . . maybe there is something in what you say," he said slowly. "She may have bumped her head a little . . . h-m-m . . . Well, I can't stay for the meeting. I must put my granddaughter to bed. I would . . . h-m-m . . . I would be very obliged to you if you would not mention anything of this talk at the meeting tonight."

"Not mention a word," said the blacksmith mayor, cheerfully.

17

The meeting in the blacksmith shop was short, quick and to the point, mainly because the village blacksmith mayor was so cheerful that night. He opened the meeting and told the frightened villagers that he already had a plan how they could fulfill the Giant's orders . . . or what the Wizard had reported were the Giant's orders.

They would borrow the wheat, barley, corn and all the other things the Giant had ordered from the friendly villagers in the neighboring valley. The blacksmith mayor, the miller and a few other good men and true, would drive their big wagons to their friendly neighbors the very next day.

And that's what they did. But their neighbors had also had
a bad year with small crops so the blacksmith mayor and the
others drove to more distant villages. At last, after four long
hot days, they returned with their big wagons only half full.
All the villagers they had visited had had a bad year with
poor crops. They had been able to borrow only about half of
what the Wizard said the Giant had ordered.

The next few days dragged by as the downcast villagers

waited for the fateful Tuesday morning when they must deliver the grain and other things halfway up the mountain. And they trembled as they drove their wagons up the mountain and unloaded the scant bushels of grain and other things. Then they drove back to their village and sat sadly in their darkened homes as they waited for the terrible things to happen which they all were sure would happen after the Giant found out they had not obeyed his orders. Some frightened villagers were sure he would tear off the roofs of their houses. Others were just as sure he would kick in their walls with one flick of his boots.

Tuesday passed! Wednesday passed! Thursday passed! And still nothing happened!

But that Friday noon just as the children were coming home for lunch, they heard in the distance the great steps of the Giant as he walked down the mountainside.

"The Giant's coming! The Giant's coming!" they screamed. And all the villagers ran for home as fast as they could. And they shuttered their windows, bolted their doors, clamped their hands to their ears and sat trembling in their dark houses as they awaited the coming of the Giant.

Everybody in the village did that except two people. One was the wicked Wizard. And the other was little Gwendolyn.

Gwendolyn had run up to her bedroom under the eaves of her grandfather's house and she threw her shutters wide open! And she did not clamp her hands tight to her ears. She wanted to hear the Giant talk. But she did protect her ears a little from the Giant's great roaring voice by wrapping a big muffler around her head and over her ears.

Closer and closer came the great earth-shaking steps of the Giant. When he reached the old cobbler's house, his face lit up with a gigantic smile. For there he saw Gwendolyn's unshuttered friendly-looking little window.

And looking out through her friendly window were the smiling rosy faces of Gwendolyn and her doll Marguerite.

"Hello, Giant!" shouted Gwendolyn in the loudest voice she could manage.

"Hello," said the Giant in the softest voice he could manage. "You need not shout. I can hear little things."

"It is a nice day," said Gwendolyn in her natural voice.

"It is a very fine day," said the Giant. "A little too hot. We do need some rain."

"Yes, indeed," said Gwendolyn. "We do indeed need rain."

Then there was a moment of silence as Gwendolyn wondered what one should say to a Giant after one says hello and talks about the weather. And the Giant wondered what one talks about to a little girl. Then he noticed the muffler wrapped around her head.

"Do you have mumps?" he asked, nodding at the muffler.

"Oh, no," said Gwendolyn. "It's just to protect my ears. You do have a strong voice, you know."

"Oh," said the Giant, sadly.

"Giant," said Gwendolyn, "I just thought of something."

"What?" asked the Giant as he knelt down.

"I believe if you raised a big thick beard like the Miller's, people could listen to your big voice without hurting their ears . . . Are you old enough to raise a beard?"

"I am old," said the Giant . . . "Yes, I guess I am old enough to raise a beard . . . And how old are you, girl?"

"Oh, I am seven going on eight," said Gwendolyn. "I have been seven going on eight for the longest time. I will be eight on Hallowe'en, October 31st."

And there was another moment of silence.

"Do you like flowers?" asked the Giant.

"I love flowers," said Gwendolyn. "But they do make me sneeze."

"Not my flowers," said the Giant. "It's the pollen that makes one sneeze and I always shake them well when I pick flowers."

The Giant opened one of his huge hands and showed Gwendolyn the flowers he carried. They were the biggest, most beautiful, purple pansies anyone had ever seen!

"How beautiful!" exclaimed Gwendolyn.

"You can have them," said the Giant, and he shoved the flowers into the little window.

"Oh, thank you, Giant," said Gwendolyn. "Wait till I put them on my bed."

24

With some difficulty she carried the big pansies to her bed.
They covered the bed from head to foot like a big purple
comforter. In a moment she was back at the window again.

"Well, goodbye," said the Giant.

"Goodbye, Giant," said Gwendolyn, "come again."

And the Giant walked back to his big black granite castle
on the top of the tremendous mountain with a happy, springy
step that shook all the little village houses like a series of earth-
quakes.

As soon as the Giant left her window Gwendolyn ran to the
door of her room and called her grandfather. The old cobbler
stumbled up the stairs as fast as he could, not knowing what
to expect.

"Look, grandfather," she cried, "look, he brought them and
he gave them all to me."

"Who brought what?" asked her grandfather.

"The Giant brought the purple pansies as he said he would
. . . Here, you can have two."

By this time the old cobbler saw the big purple pansies
spread out on Gwendolyn's bed.

"So he did . . . so he did," was all he could say. Then as
he looked at the two pansies Gwendolyn had laid in his hands
he said, "I never saw such pansies . . ."

Gwendolyn chattered on and on telling about the Giant's
visit and what they had talked about. Her grandfather listened
carefully. Then he sat down deep in thought.

As usual, right after a visit from the Giant the wicked Wizard
read his report on what he said the Giant had ordered. This
time he told the villagers the Giant was very angry and he
again read off a list of orders that the unhappy villagers knew
they never could fulfill. And as usual everything must be

26

delivered halfway up the mountain by Tuesday noon . . . no later.

Gwendolyn and her grandfather stood at the edge of the crowd and listened to the wicked Wizard's report but they said not a word to anyone.

That evening right after supper the old cobbler put some things in a sack, threw the sack over his shoulder and again he hurried over to the blacksmith shop before the regular meeting of the villagers.

The blacksmith mayor let him in the door. He was very distressed.

"Please, my old friend, not tonight," he said. "Please do not tell me of the bright fantastic things your granddaughter said. I know . . . I know she is a very remarkable, very imaginative child. But please, not tonight, there are so many serious . . ."

"I did not come to tell you anything," interrupted the old cobbler, "I came to show you something."

Then the old cobbler reached into the sack he had carried on his shoulder and he pulled out two big shoes.

"Here are your shoes," he said. "I mended them and I am delivering them."

"Shoes! . . . Shoes!" roared the blacksmith. "Here we are faced with the worst catastrophe this village has ever known . . . and you come showing me shoes."

"They are your shoes," said the old cobbler.

The blacksmith picked up his mended shoes and looked at the soles with an impatient frown. Then he looked into them.

"What's this?" he cried. "What's this purple lining you've put in my shoes . . . What do you mean . . ."

"*That* is not a purple lining," said the cobbler. "Look again."

The blacksmith looked and then he reached his hand into one of his shoes and picked out a large purple pansy. He reached into the other and pulled out another purple pansy.

"Purple pansies!" he gasped.

"Yes, purple pansies," said the cobbler. "And pansies this big do not grow any place in this valley . . . Do you want to know where they came from? I'll tell you!"

In a few minutes the old cobbler told the blacksmith everything Gwendolyn had told him about the Giant's visit.

That evening the regular meeting of the villagers at the blacksmith shop was over even quicker than the last meeting. The blacksmith mayor said he knew of a large secret store of grain and all of the other things the Giant wanted. All he would need was a number of good strong silent men to help and he would guarantee everything would be taken care of by Tuesday. Then he chose the biggest, strongest men in the village. Everyone knew these men never gossiped and never told any secrets. He arranged to hold a special secret meeting. The Wizard was not invited.

The following Tuesday, promptly at noon, the blacksmith and the strong, silent men he had chosen drove halfway up the mountain and they unloaded hundreds of baskets of what looked like good grain and other things, exactly as the Wizard had said the Giant had ordered.

But those baskets were not full of good grain . . . Oh, no. They were just full of twigs and pebbles. And each basket was covered with a cloth sprinkled with just a handful of grain. Late that night when the wicked Wizard and his servants loaded the baskets on their own wagons and carted them away to the secret cave where they had hidden all the other things the Giant was supposed to have ordered, the blacksmith and his chosen men followed them as silent as panthers.

There, armed with great homemade clubs, the villagers

quickly subdued the wicked Wizard and his villainous servants. And all the grain and cattle and sheep that had been stolen from the villagers and hidden in the secret cave were returned to their rightful owners.

Naturally, the wicked Wizard and his servants (all of them ex-robbers, ex-pirates, and ex-bandits) were driven from that peaceful little valley and were never seen again.

The villagers settled back again to a peaceful, prosperous, carefree life. Now that they knew that the Giant was really a gentle, amiable fellow (because Gwendolyn had said so and her grandfather had told everyone else) the villagers looked forward to the next visit of their gigantic neighbor.

And they went to some trouble to show the Giant he was welcome in their village. They decorated the fronts of their houses with colored streamers and flags. And Gwendolyn and the other children lettered a big sign that was stretched across the village street. The sign read, "Welcome Giant."

And when all that was done, they sat back and waited. And they waited . . . and they waited . . . and they waited! But weeks went by, months went by and still there was no visit from the Giant. The decorations became tattered, the flags were limp and the big sign the children had printed looked washed out and shaggy. And just as the villagers were beginning to think that perhaps they had hurt his feelings and that he might never visit them again, along came the Giant!

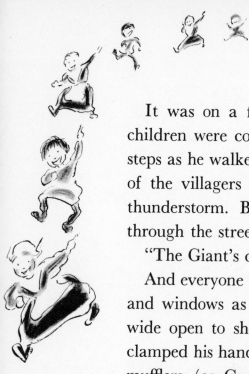

It was on a fine, warm Indian summer day. Just as the children were coming home from school they heard his great steps as he walked down from his tremendous mountain. Some of the villagers thought it was the sound of a late summer thunderstorm. But the children knew better. They danced through the street shouting . . .

"The Giant's coming! . . . The Giant's coming!"

And everyone ran for home. This time not to bolt their doors and windows as they had formerly done, but to throw them wide open to show the Giant he was welcome. And no one clamped his hands to his ears. They all wrapped their heads in mufflers (as Gwendolyn said they should do) to muffle the sound of the Giant's great voice so that they could hear what he said.

At last along came the Giant.

He was very pleasantly surprised to find all the village doors and windows open wide and to see all the villagers and the children looking out and smiling as they nodded him a good-day. He stepped over the sign that the children had printed and stopped again at the old cobbler's house. There he knelt and looked into Gwendolyn's window.

If it were not for the size of him and his kindly twinkling eyes, Gwendolyn would have hardly recognized her Giant friend. For the rest of the Giant's great face was almost all covered with a gigantic red beard and a tremendous moustache!

"Hello," said the Giant. His voice now coming through his great beard and moustache was so deep and mellow Gwendolyn could hardly hear him.

She quickly unwrapped the muffler she had tied around her head to protect her ears and she did the same for her doll Marguerite.

"Hello, Giant," said Gwendolyn, "I missed you . . . Have you been sick?"

"No," said the Giant, with a sheepish grin, "I have been raising this beard."

"It is a beautiful beard," said Gwendolyn.

The Giant blushed at her compliment and for a moment there was a silence between them.

"Nice day we're having," said the Giant at last.

"It is a beautiful day indeed," said Gwendolyn.

Then after another pause the Giant said:

"Did you not tell me that October 31st was your birthday?"

"How nice of you to remember," said Gwendolyn with a surprised look on her face. "Yes, October 31st, tomorrow, is my birthday. I'll be eight."

"Well," said the Giant, slowly. "I'd like to have you and all the children come halfway up the mountain tomorrow . . . I'm making a birthday party for you . . . I baked a cake."

"Oh, how kind and thoughtful you are, Giant," said Gwendolyn, joyfully. "I'd love a birthday party up on the mountain."

And so it happened on the very next day when Gwendolyn, who had been seven going on eight for the longest time, finally became eight years old on October 31st (Hallowe'en) the Giant spread a great cloth halfway up on the mountainside and on it he laid great platters. These platters held more goose-berry tarts, more cookies, more sugarplums and candies than anyone had ever seen. And right in the center of the cloth was the cake the Giant had baked *himself*! It was the biggest homemade, pink-frosted birthday cake in the world with eight candles and one to grow on, stuck in the center of it.

The village children came to the party all dressed up in Hallowe'en costumes. Some boys came dressed as girls and some girls came dressed as boys. And some children were goblins and others were witches and there were those who pretended to be black cats and even pumpkins. But *no one* came dressed as a *Wizard*.

And they all ate as much as they could hold and they played games and sang, "Happy Birthday, dear Gwendolyn," over and over again. And that was the song they sang as they walked down the mountain when the sun set and it was time to go home to bed.

Everyone said that the birthday party the amiable Giant gave for Gwendolyn when she became eight years old was the best party that ever was.

And that still holds true to this very day!

If anyone has any doubts about that, all he need do is to go visit that little village in the valley at the foot of the tremendous mountain. He is sure to meet some very old people sitting around in the sunny village square. And they will tell him that it is true, because their great-great-great grandfathers and great-great-grandmothers had been guests at that gigantic birthday party for Gwendolyn, the cobbler's granddaughter. And these very old people when they tell this story will point to the exact spot in the village square where there once was an old dried-up well into which Gwendolyn tumbled. And then, they will point with their canes to the tremendous mountain, now crowned with great, billowy, white clouds where the amiable Giant lived in his big black, granite castle a long, long, long time ago.

THE END